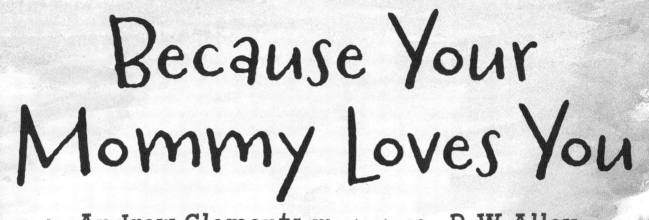

Because Your Mommy Loves You

by **Andrew Clements** Illustrated by **R. W. Alley**

CLARION BOOKS
Houghton Mifflin Harcourt
Boston • New York •

Clarion Books

215 Park Avenue South

New York, New York 10003

Text copyright © 2012 by Andrew Clements

Illustrations copyright © 2012 by R. W. Alley

Clarion Books is an imprint of Houghton Mifflin Harcourt Publishing Company.

www.hmhbooks.com

The text of this book was set in 19-point Billy Serif.

The illustrations were executed in ink, watercolor, and acrylic.

Library of Congress Cataloging-in-Publication Data is available.

LCCN 2011025594

Manufactured in China

LEO 10 9 8 7 6 5 4 3 2

4500358322

For Kathy Brault, a dear friend and a great mom
—A.C.

For Zoë, are our kids lucky or what?
—R.W.A.

WHEN you get lost in the camping store, and you call out,

Mommy!

your mommy could say,
It's all right, I'm coming to find you!
But she doesn't.

TENTS

Sleeping
Bags

MAPS

COAST

MOUNTAINS

BOATS

BUY
LOTS OF
STUFF

7

She calls your name,

and you follow the sound of her voice.

When you find her, you get a big hug—
after you promise not to wander off again.

When the pack on your back
feels like a giant rock,

your mommy could say,
That looks awfully heavy
for you. Here, I'll carry it!
But she doesn't.

You both sit down a while
and share some water
and a handful of raisins.

Then she helps you strap on
your pack again,
and up the trail you go.

When you have to cross the stream,
and the log looks skinny and wobbly,

your mommy could say,
Don't worry, I'll take you across.
But she doesn't.

TRAIL

15

She goes over first to show you how.
And then you follow, all by yourself.

When you find a blueberry patch,
and it takes forever to fill one tiny cup,

your mommy could say,
Oh, don't bother—you've
done plenty.
But she doesn't.

She shows you where to find the best bushes,
and how to use your hat like a bowl.
And soon you have enough to make
blueberry pancakes.

When it's time to set up the tent,
and your side gets all tangled up,

your mommy could say,
This is a job for a grownup—let me fix it for you.
But she doesn't.

She shows you the pictures again. Then, step by step,
the poles and cloth and rope become . . .

... your tent!

When your marshmallow gets too close to the fire
and turns into a lump of charcoal,

your mommy could say,
What a shame!
Here, I'll make you
one that's just right.
But she doesn't.

She helps you find a stick shaped like a Y.
She shows you how to push it into the ground
beside the fire.
And your next marshmallow
is toasty-licious!

When the fire burns low,
and you see five shooting stars,
and it gets so cold you start to shiver,

your mommy could say,
Stay right there—I'll get you something cozy.
But she doesn't.

She hands you a flashlight
and reminds you where
you left your sweatshirt.

You go into the dark tent,

and after you find it,
you pull it on
and hurry back to the fire.

And the two of you
snuggle extra close.

When it's very late,
and you can barely keep your eyes open,

your mommy could say,
You're all tuckered out. Let me carry you to bed.
But she doesn't.

She pulls you up,
and you help her put out the fire.
She follows you to the tent,
and you crawl in first.

While you take your boots off,
she fluffs up your pillow
and unrolls your sleeping bag.
You slide inside,

and she zips the zipper up to your chin.

And then your mommy could say,
See you when the sun comes up!

or

Lots more hiking tomorrow!

or

Get a good rest, now!

But she doesn't.

She whispers,

Snowball the Wonder Dog

by Cindy West
illustrated by Pat Paris

A GOLDEN BOOK • NEW YORK
Western Publishing Company, Inc., Racine, Wisconsin 53404

One rainy night Dabney Nabbit, the dogcatcher, brought a little brown dog to the Pound. He shivered with fear as Nabbit tossed him in, locked the gate, and left.

"*Ah-ooo!*" howled the dog. His cries were so loud that they woke Cooler, who was sleeping nearby.

"Poor little guy!" said Cooler. "Who are you? Do you live around here?"

"No," said the newcomer. "I'm a circus dog. Tonight I was practicing backward somersaults on the circus train. The next thing I knew I was lying in the mud. That's when the dogcatcher caught me."

"Well, you came to the right place," said Cooler. "The Pound Puppies will help you get back to the circus. But first, how about a shower and some supper?"

"That sounds terrific," said the new dog gratefully.

Cooler woke Scrounger, who searched through his supplies and found a shower hose. He hooked it up to the tap and aimed it at the little dog.

"Hey," Scrounger said. "You're not brown. You're white."

"Of course. I'm Snowball the Wonder Dog."

"Well, how about that?" said Scrounger.

When morning came, Cooler and Scrounger introduced
Snowball to The Nose and Barkerville.

"This is our team," Cooler said. "It's time to make our
escape."

"Escape? But how?" asked Snowball.

"Watch," said Cooler. "We do it almost every day."

Cooler led Snowball and the others to a spot near the Pound fence. Unfortunately, Itchey and Snitchey, the two guard dogs, were too close for comfort.

"What'll we do now?" asked Snowball.

"Watch," said Cooler.

RING·RING·RING·RING

Scrounger disappeared for a minute and came back with a
hat that looked exactly like Dabney Nabbit's. He propped it
on top of some packing crates so that only the back could
be seen. Then he had one of the other Pound Puppies ring
the dinner bell.

Itchey and Snitchey went running toward Nabbit's hat, thinking he was bringing them food. The Pound Puppies and Snowball crawled through a secret tunnel under the fence.

The puppies came out by a fire hydrant at the other end
of the tunnel.

"Now where do we go?" asked Snowball.

"The circus needs a big field to set up in," said
Barkerville, "probably near the edge of town."

"Why don't we all form a line like the elephants in the
circus?" suggested Snowball.

"Great!" said The Nose. "I'll lead the way and try to sniff out circus smells like sawdust, popcorn, and hot dogs. Speaking of hot dogs," she continued excitedly, "I smell some right now."

Quickly she led them to...

...Violet Vanderfeller's yard. Violet invited all her old friends to join her cookout. The Pound Puppies ate hot dogs until they were full. Then Violet joined them as they rushed off in search of the circus.

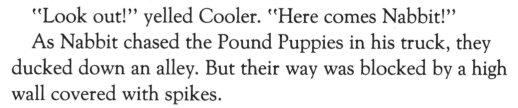

"Look out!" yelled Cooler. "Here comes Nabbit!"
As Nabbit chased the Pound Puppies in his truck, they ducked down an alley. But their way was blocked by a high wall covered with spikes.

Scrounger looked around for something they could use to escape. There was nothing but some old mattresses.

"I'll show you how to escape," said Snowball. "It's an old circus trick."

First, the Pound Puppies threw a mattress over the wall so it leaned against the other side. Then they put up another mattress on their side of the wall.

Snowball raced up the mattress, digging his claws in.
Then he let go and somersaulted down the other side.
"Cool!" said Cooler. All the Pound Puppies ran up and
did somersaults too.

When they were safely away from Nabbit, The Nose said,
"I smell popcorn. We *must* be near the circus." She led
them straight to...a movie theater.

"Try again," Cooler urged. The Nose sniffed and then she
sneezed—*ah-choo!* "I smell sawdust," she said.

And she led the Pound Puppies straight to...

...the circus!

"Welcome back, Snowball!" said the man at the gate. "Everyone has been looking for you! Hurry, it's almost showtime. The rest of you have to stay here because you're not performers."

"Not yet," Cooler whispered to Snowball. "Go on in and get into your costume. We'll find a way to come and help you do your act. Just bark when you want us."

Scrounger found a bunch of paper cupcake cups at a bakery. Quickly he put them on all the puppies' necks.

"Very proper circus collars!" said Barkerville. "I feel rather like a circus dog myself."

Snowball raced over to his owner, Miss Elise Lee, and licked her face. He tried to tell her that soon she would be meeting his friends from the Pound. But she didn't understand his barks and growls, and was just happy Snowball was back.

Snowball put on his costume and he and Elise Lee entered the center ring. Everyone clapped and cheered.

"*Ar-rufff!*" Snowball gave a special bark, and the Pound Puppies rushed into the ring. They built a big pyramid with Snowball the Wonder Dog at the top. The Pound Puppies were the hit of the whole show!

When their act was over, the Pound Puppies went backstage and met the elephants and the horses—and even the clowns.

Suddenly Nabbit rushed in. "I've got you now," he growled to the Pound Puppies.

"*Gr-roar!*" Leo the Lion growled back.

"Help!" Nabbit cried, and he ran right back to his truck.

The Pound Puppies ate lots of popcorn and cotton candy.

"Well," Cooler said, "now I think it's time to catch up with Nabbit."

"You mean you *want* to go back to the Pound?" Snowball asked with surprise.

"Yes," said Cooler. "If we weren't there, who would find homes for the other puppies that Nabbit brings in?"

Snowball said good-bye to his Pound Puppy friends. He promised to tell them when the circus was coming back again.

Cooler grinned as the Pound Puppies rode off in Nabbit's truck. He was already wondering about the next mission he and his friends would go on...finding a home for another Pound Puppy.